THE SAN FRANCISCO EARTHQUAKE, 1906

I SURVIVED

I SURVIVED

THE SAN FRANCISCO EARTHQUAKE, 1906

by Lauren Tarshis

illustrated by Scott Dawson

Scholastic Inc.

NEW YORK TORONTO LONDON AUCKLAND
SYDNEY MEXICO CITY NEW DELHI HONG KONG

No part of this publication may be reproduced, stored in a retrieval system, or transmitted in any form or by any means, electronic, mechanical, photocopying, recording, or otherwise, without written permission of the publisher. For information regarding permission, write to Scholastic Inc., Attention: Permissions Department, 557 Broadway, New York, NY 10012.

ISBN 978-0-545-20699-0

29

17/0

40

Printed in the U.S.A.
First printing, January 2012
Designed by Tim Hall

FOR VALERIE

CHAPTER 1

APRIL 18, 1906

RINCON HILL

5:12 A.M.

SAN FRANCISCO, CALIFORNIA

The sky was still dark when the ground began to shake.

Most people in San Francisco were still sleeping. Just a few were awake. Shopkeepers arranged their stores, getting ready for the day.

Carriage drivers fed their horses. Newsboys ran down the sidewalk to pick up their newspapers to sell.

And eleven-year-old Leo Ross was in a broken-down building, high on Rincon Hill.

When the rumbling started, Leo thought it might be thunder. He had no idea that deep below the city, two gigantic pieces of earth were pushing past each other. Powerful shocks exploded up through the underground layers of dirt and rock. All across the city, streets ripped open. Buildings swayed. Walls crumbled and houses came crashing down. Broken glass, hunks of wood, and piles of bricks tumbled into the streets.

Leo stood in shock as the floor beneath him rose and fell like ocean waves. Hunks of plaster hit him on the head. Windows shattered, spraying glass all around.

He tried to scream, but his throat was coated with dust.

He wanted to run, but he couldn't even stand.
The shaking was too hard.

And then there was a sound like an explosion.
The ceiling above his head burst open.

A brick hit him, *smack*, on the back.

And then another, *thud*, hit him in the shoulder.

Crash!

Dozens of bricks poured down.

Leo fell to the floor and curled into a ball.

The bricks kept coming, raining down.

He couldn't see.

He couldn't breathe.

Soon he would be buried alive.

CHAPTER 2

20 HOURS EARLIER

"President Roosevelt is coming to town!" Leo shouted. "Read all about it!"

Leo was standing on his corner, selling that morning's newspaper. The sidewalk was crowded with men rushing to work. They barely slowed down as they handed Leo their nickels and grabbed the newspapers from his hands.

It was barely 7:00 in the morning, and Leo

had sold almost all of his papers. He jingled his pockets, which were heavy with coins. He thought about the fresh roll he'd buy for breakfast. And maybe even some cold milk to wash it down with.

He smiled to himself.

Papa would have been proud of him.

Leo patted his right-hand trouser pocket and felt the gold nugget that he always kept with him.

It didn't look like much — kind of like a chewed-up yellow rock. But it was worth a fortune, Leo knew. Probably he could get more money for it than he earned in months of selling papers.

But he'd rather sell his heart than this gold nugget.

Leo's grandfather had found it in a riverbed east of here, during the gold rush.

He'd handed it down to Papa, who had carried it with him everywhere. Grandpop got sick and died before Leo was born. But Papa kept him alive through the stories he'd tell to Leo. Each night, when Papa was putting Leo to bed, he'd take out the gold nugget. Leo would hold it tight in his hand as Papa told tales of Grandpop's adventures — crossing America all alone in a creaky old wagon, almost getting eaten by a giant grizzly in the Rocky Mountains, surviving a forest fire in the Sierras, living in San Francisco when it was just a bunch of rickety houses in the mud.

"You're just like your grandpop," Papa always said. "I see it in your eyes. You've got his good luck. You've got his guts. Something remarkable is going to happen to you. I can feel it, can't you?"

And the way Papa would look at him, with shining eyes, Leo did feel it.

These past few months since the fever took Papa away, there had been days when sadness would surround Leo, a feeling as cold and gray as the San Francisco fog. He'd feel scared, and very alone. He'd miss Papa so bad, his whole body would hurt.

But then he would think of Grandpop, who made his way from New Hampshire to California all by himself, when he was just sixteen years old. And he'd hear Papa's voice in his mind, bright and clear, telling him that he was lucky, and brave, and that something remarkable was going to happen to him.

Papa's voice was loud and clear on this sunny day.

Or it was, until Leo finished selling papers.

He was walking down an alley, cutting through to Market Street.

Somehow he didn't notice the two boys who had crept up behind him.

Next thing Leo knew, he'd been smashed against a brick wall, and blood was gushing out of his nose.

CHAPTER 3

"Hand it over," said a raspy voice.

Leo didn't have to see the face to know who was talking.

It was Fletch Sikes, the most brutal thief in the neighborhood. The other kid had to be Wilkie Barnes, a giant of a boy who went everywhere Fletch did.

When Fletch was just five years old, the story went, he'd been attacked by a pack of stray dogs. He'd survived, but one of the dogs had bitten his throat. The bite ruined his voice. And turned Fletch vicious.

Fletch and Wilkie didn't just steal food and pick pockets.

Sometimes they beat kids up just for fun.

A few months ago, they'd been caught by the police, and sent to a work farm up north.

Leo had heard a rumor that they had escaped. He'd heard that they were hiding out in an old, abandoned saloon on Rincon Hill.

And now here they were, back to their old vicious tricks.

"You can take my money," Leo said, trying not to sound as terrified as he felt.

"We don't want your money," Wilkie said. The kid was a monster. He had to weigh almost three hundred pounds, with smooth chubby cheeks like a baby.

A baby with a steel fist.

"What do you want?" Leo asked, his knees shaking.

"You know," Fletch growled.

Leo's heart stopped. Of course he knew.

Somehow Fletch had found out about Leo's gold nugget.

But how?

Leo hadn't told a soul about it.

Except . . .

Morris. That little pest of a kid, who buzzed around Leo like a fly.

Leo had showed him the gold a few weeks ago. He must have blabbed about it to kids on the street. And the story had gotten back to Fletch and Wilkie.

Fletch pushed Leo's face harder into the wall. The bones of Leo's cheek felt like they would crack, like the shell of an egg.

"Take my money," Leo said again. "I have more than a dollar. Take it all."

"We will," Fletch said, with a rasping laugh. "But we want the gold, too."

Hand it over.

It was Papa's voice, in Leo's head.

Leo knew there was no way he could fight these guys, no way to outrun them. Wilkie was the fastest kid in the neighborhood.

But that gold had been Papa's prized possession. Leo couldn't just give it up.

"No," Leo said, summoning up all of his strength. He whirled around and broke free from Fletch's grip.

He made it about three steps before Wilkie caught him by the back of the shirt, and threw him onto the ground.

Slam!

Leo landed hard, biting his tongue.

"Hand it over!" Fletch shouted in his creepy, strangled voice.

"No!" Leo yelled again.

What happened next took only a minute. Wilkie picked Leo up by his shirt, holding him in the air as Fletch emptied Leo's pockets. Then

Wilkie threw him into a pile of garbage. The two goons walked away, laughing.

Blood dribbled from Leo's mouth.

His head throbbed.

But the worst was the searing pain from somewhere deep inside, like something had been ripped out of him.

His gold was gone.

CHAPTER 4

Leo had no idea how much time passed.

And then a voice calling his name woke him from his daze.

Papa?

"Leo! Leo Ross! Where are you?"

Leo groaned to himself.

Morris.

Why did that kid constantly pester him? From the first day they'd met, Morris had acted like they were long lost brothers. They both lived

14

in the same boardinghouse, Leo by himself in a tiny basement room, Morris upstairs with his uncle, a sweaty man with a huge stomach who yelled at the little girls when they played dolls on the boardinghouse steps. Every day when Leo got home, Morris was waiting for him at the front door. The kid worked at a grocery, but he spent every spare second at the public library. He always had some new fact to share with Leo.

"Leo, you know that rat that lives under the front steps? Did you know its Latin name is *Rattus rattus*?"

"Leo, did you know that this neighborhood used to be a swamp? They filled it in with garbage and old wood and then built these buildings."

"Leo, did you know that the San Francisco library has a million books?"

In Leo's heart, he knew that Morris just wanted to be pals. But Leo didn't need any friends. He especially didn't need a friend like Morris, a skinny twerp who didn't know when to shut up. A kid like that wouldn't do Leo any good.

What had Leo been thinking when he showed Morris his gold?

He thought back to that night a few weeks ago, when Leo had seen Morris sitting alone on the steps of the cigar store near their boarding-house. At first Leo figured he could sneak by and escape Morris for one day. But something was wrong with the kid. And Leo just couldn't walk by without seeing what it was.

It took Leo some time to get Morris to spit out what was wrong — that his uncle was hardly ever home, that he gambled all of his money away, including the few dimes a day Morris earned at the market.

"I have to get out of here," Morris said. "My ma has cousins in New York City. I met them once. You'd love them, Leo! They're both teachers. They said I could go to their school. They always said I was welcome there anytime."

"Why don't you just go?" Leo said.

Then finally Leo could live in peace!

"How?" Morris said. "I don't have the money to get on a train. My uncle just laughs when I mention it. I'm trapped here."

There was no cheering Morris up—until Leo reached into his pocket and took out his gold. He handed it to Morris, like Papa used to hand it to him.

Morris's eyes almost popped out of his head.

Leo told him about Grandpop, and how people laughed when he used to talk about one day crossing the wild country by himself. Of course Leo knew that Morris was nothing like Grandpop. But the story worked like a charm.

What was Morris doing out on the streets looking for him now? Couldn't he mind his own business for one day? Morris was the reason he'd just lost his gold to Fletch and Wilkie, the reason he was lying bleeding in the alley. Morris was the last person Leo wanted to see.

Leo kept quiet, hoping that Morris would move along.

But no, Morris kept at it. And suddenly there he was, crouched down next to Leo.

"I've been looking everywhere for you," he said. "I knew something must have happened!"

Morris took out a handkerchief and started wiping the caked blood from Leo's face.

"Whoever did this to you," Morris fumed, "I swear I'll get them!"

Leo would have laughed, but his jaw was too sore.

"It was Fletch Sikes and Wilkie Barnes," Leo mumbled. "They stole my gold."

Morris gasped.

"You were the only person who knew about it," Leo added.

"I didn't tell Fletch Sikes about your gold!" Morris said.

"But you told someone, right?" Leo said.

Morris's shoulders slumped.

"I might have mentioned it to some kids at the market," he said. "It was such a great story, and I . . . well, it really got their attention."

Leo shook his head. The kid was so desperate for friends he'd spilled Leo's most important secret. He should clobber him.

But no person could look sorrier than Morris looked now.

Leo sighed. Being mad at Morris wasn't going to get his gold back.

He let Morris help him stand up. Together they made their way back to the boardinghouse.

Morris jabbered the entire way.

"I'm going to help you get that gold back," he said, as they stepped through the front door.

"It will be sold by tomorrow," Leo said.

Morris frowned. "I know," Morris said. "That's why we need to get it back tonight."

"We?" Leo said. Now he had to laugh. Morris really thought he stood a chance next to Fletch and Wilkie?

"Of course they won't just *give* it back," Morris said, ignoring Leo's question. "We have to trick them somehow."

Leo looked at Morris. And right then Morris didn't look like such a skinny little twerp. There was a look on his face — a thoughtful and stubborn kind of look — that reminded Leo of the way President Roosevelt appeared on the front page of today's paper. The only thing missing was the bushy mustache.

But what did Morris really know about the world? There were no books in the library about kids like Fletch and Wilkie.

Leo thanked Morris. And before Morris could say another word, Leo hurried down to his tiny basement room, slamming the door behind him.

CHAPTER 5

Leo sat down on the flea-bitten horse blanket that he used as a bed.

He rubbed his sore jaw. His stomach grumbled.

The best thing, he realized, would be to close his eyes, get to sleep, and forget about this day.

He closed his eyes.

But kept thinking about what Morris had said.

We could trick them.

The words had wormed their way into his mind.

Finally Leo sat up and lit a candle.

Maybe Morris was onto something. Of course Leo couldn't make those two goons hand over the gold. But maybe there *was* a way to trick them.

Like the way Grandpop had tricked the grizzly bear.

Leo could hear Papa's voice now in his mind, telling the story.

It was 1849, and Grandpop was only sixteen years old.

Gold had been discovered in a streambed in northern California, and Grandpop was heading west to make his fortune. It had been a tough journey. He'd been held up by bandits near St. Louis. He came *this close* to getting bitten by a four-foot-long rattlesnake in the Indian Territory. Finally he'd made it high into the Rocky Mountains. It was rough country, but beautiful too, with streams as blue as the sky and fields of wildflowers that stretched out like rainbows.

The sun was setting, and Grandpop had made his camp and built his fire. He got up to fetch some wood for the night. He was coming back over a hill when he saw an enormous bear. "Three times the size of a man," Papa would say, stretching his arms up to the ceiling.

The bear rose up and roared at Grandpop, baring enormous teeth.

Grandpop knew about the Rocky Mountain grizzlies. They ran faster than mountain lions. They could climb trees. They could rip a person to shreds with a swipe of a paw. Grandpop could see the bear's claws, ten black daggers glistening in the setting sun.

The bear stood there, ready to attack.

All Grandpop wanted to do was run. But no one can outrun a grizzly. They're too fast.

All travelers are told this. And yet most men can't help themselves. The urge to run is just too strong to resist.

But Grandpop wasn't like other men.

Every muscle in his body was ready to run.

But he planted his feet into the ground.

Think, he told himself. *Think.*

He couldn't escape from that grizzly bear. He couldn't kill the grizzly. His gun was in his tent.

His only hope was to scare that grizzly away.

But how?

And then Grandpop remembered:

The rattle.

The rattle of that monster rattlesnake he'd killed in Pawnee Indian land.

The snake was as thick as Grandpop's leg. Its rattle was five inches long.

That snake could have killed him. He'd almost stepped on it when he was walking through the tall plains grass, hunting for rabbits. By the time Grandpop heard the rattling noise, the snake was coiled and ready to strike.

Shkshkshkshkshkshkshkshkshkshk,

shkshkshkshkshkshkshkshkshkshk,

shkshkshkshkshkshkshkshkshkshk.

Without a thought, Grandpop had grabbed his knife from his belt and threw it. By some stroke of luck, the blade landed in the center of the snake's head.

The snake didn't die right away. It thrashed wildly, its body coiling around Grandpop's legs. Grandpop had to hit it with the handle of his rifle.

And then, when the snake was dead, Grandpop cut off the rattle for good luck.

Far from those tall grasses in the prairie, the grizzly bear snarled at Grandpop, inching closer.

Grandpop put his hand in his pocket and started shaking the snake's rattle. The sound rose up around them.

Shkshkshkshkshkshkshkshkshkshkshk,
    shkshkshkshkshkshkshkshkshkshkshk,
    shkshkshkshkshkshkshkshkshkshkshk.

Grandpop hoped that grizzlies were afraid of rattlesnakes. He hoped he could trick it into thinking that he was some kind of huge rattlesnake-man. A fearsome monster.

The bear looked around, and Grandpop could see the fear in its eyes.

It let off one last roar, and then scampered off.

Now, sitting on his flea-bitten blanket, Leo realized that Morris was right. There might be a way to scare Fletch and Wilkie, to trick them into giving back the gold just like Grandpop had tricked that bear into running away.

And sure enough, sometime in the middle of the night, Leo had come up with a plan.

CHAPTER 6

What gave Leo his idea was a story that every kid in San Francisco knew, a ghost story about a man named Corey Drew.

He was a man who had struck it rich during the gold rush and moved to San Francisco. He'd lived in Rincon Hill, which was the fanciest part of San Francisco back then. He was all set to build himself a huge mansion, marry a fine lady, and start his new life.

Then one night, walking up Rincon Hill, he was robbed and stabbed to death.

His killer was never found.

But old-timers said that his ghost still haunted the streets of that neighborhood.

Leo wasn't afraid of Corey Drew. Some kids were scared to be on Rincon Hill after dark. There was even a creepy rhyme about it, which every kid in San Francisco knew as well as the ABCs.

On Rincon Hill, way up high
There lived a man who would not die
Corey Drew, Corey Drew
Is watching you, is watching you.
Corey Drew, Corey Drew
See a crow and then you're through.
Late at night, shine no light.
Or you might just die of fright.

Leo knew that Fletch and Wilkie weren't afraid of him or any other kids.

They weren't afraid of the police.

But just maybe, they were a little afraid of the ghost of Corey Drew.

Leo's idea was to make Fletch and Wilkie believe that Corey Drew had come to get them. Leo had a tattered old hat of Papa's. He had a tin of flour, which he would rub on his face for a deathly look. He had a candle, which he would hold under his chin to give himself a ghostly glow.

He'd talk in a low whisper.

"Give me my gold!" he'd say.

With their eyes full of sleep, hopefully Fletch and Wilkie would believe that they really could be looking at a ghost. And they'd be just scared enough to hand over the gold nugget.

Leo knew it was a crazy idea, for sure.

But no crazier than scaring away a hungry grizzly with a cut-off snake rattle.

It was past 4:30 A.M. when Leo set out for Rincon Hill.

He'd decided to go close to sunrise. He needed darkness for his plan to work. But in case something had happened with Fletch, Leo wanted there to be some people out on the streets. He'd know right away if Fletch and Wilkie were falling for his trick. And if they didn't, he'd have to get away quickly.

But Leo didn't see a soul as he walked through the narrow streets up toward Rincon Hill. He heard some curses from the alleys—gamblers, probably. A baby's cry sounded from an open window. A milk wagon rattled by.

But the streets were deserted.

Except for the dogs. They seemed to be everywhere Leo looked. Darting in and out of doorways, sprinting across the streets, shivering against buildings. Their howls and cries filled the air.

Aaaaaoooooooooooooooooooooooooooo!

Aaaaaoooooooooooooooooooooooooooo!

He'd never heard such a sound before.

He wondered what was upsetting the dogs. Papa had said that Grandpop always listened to the cries of wolves.

"They always know when there's danger around."

Did the dogs know something that Leo didn't?

Were they trying to tell him he should run home?

Don't be stupid, Leo told himself. Maybe the dogs howled like this every night when Leo was fast asleep. He was letting the darkness get to him.

He reminded himself of something Papa always said: Brave people got spooked all the time. What made them brave was that they didn't let their fear stop them. Leo thought of the noises Grandpop would have heard in the Rocky Mountains—the screams of mountain lions and the screeches of owls, gunshots of bandits and murderers. Had Grandpop let those sounds scare him off?

Heck no!

He'd kept moving forward.

And so did Leo.

Rincon Hill wasn't fancy anymore. Most of the big mansions had been turned into boarding-houses. Other streets were lined with little wooden houses, all crammed together like teeth in a crooked smile.

Leo reached the corner of Essex and Folsom, and saw a beaten-up building. The roof was half caved in. The huge chimney loomed against the black sky. The front window was shattered and the front door was hanging off its hinges.

Was this the place?

It had to be, he decided. The other buildings were just regular houses.

Leo stood on the steps, knowing that he could lose his nerve any second.

He took a deep breath, pushed aside the front door, and slipped in.

He lit his candle and held it in front of him.

He'd always imagined Fletch and Wilkie's hideout would be like a pirate den. He pictured velvet couches and fine rugs stolen from mansions on Nob Hill.

But the place was a dump. There were broken chairs and tables piled in one corner and garbage heaped in the other. The air was cold and damp, and it stunk like trash and rats. He saw two shapes sprawled across the floor, at the back of the saloon.

Leo crept closer.

It was Fletch and Wilkie, fast asleep.

They didn't even have an old horse blanket to share. They had covered themselves with newspapers. Amazing, Leo thought. This place was worse than his little room at the boarding-house.

He looked around, hoping that maybe he'd see

his gold nugget. There was a dead mouse lying stiffly near Wilkie's foot. But no gold.

Gathering up every ounce of courage he'd ever had, he put the candle under his chin. He closed his eyes and thought of Grandpop.

"Give me my gold," he whispered.

And then louder.

"Give me my gold!"

CHAPTER 7

Fletch opened his eyes first. "What the . . ." He jumped up.

Leo's candle gave the room an eerie golden glow.

Wilkie stirred for a second, grumbled, and then closed his eyes again.

Fletch gave him a cruel kick in his side.

"What?" Wilkie said, scrambling to his feet. He quickly fixed his eyes on Leo. "Who's that?"

"Give me my gold," Leo whispered again.

The two boys stared at him.

And then Leo saw it, in Wilkie's eyes.

A flicker of fear.

"It's that man!" Wilkie said.

"What man?" Fletch rasped.

"Let's get out of here," Wilkie said.

Fletch wavered a little, Leo could see. But he was still looking at Leo with a hard, untrusting expression.

He wasn't fooled, Leo thought.

This wasn't working.

Run! he told himself. *Get out of here now!*

But somehow Leo was able to stay still. He stood a little taller. He imagined he really *was* the ghost of a murdered man. Fletch and Wilkie weren't killers, as far as Leo knew. But they had hurt dozens of people in their lives, probably more. If anyone deserved to be haunted, it was these two.

"I know what you've done," Leo whispered, the way Papa used to whisper when he told his late-night stories. "You will be punished."

Wilkie looked terrified. It was as though Leo had cast a spell on him.

But then there was a loud crash from the front.

They all turned. And for a second Leo expected to see the ghost of Corey Drew hovering in the doorway.

Instead, he saw a familiar skinny shape.

Morris.

Leo's heart dropped into his boots.

Fletch let out a rasping laugh.

He walked over and grabbed Morris. He dragged him back by the collar and then pushed him hard into Leo. Leo's candle dropped to the floor. Now it was almost completely dark in the old saloon.

But that didn't stop Fletch and Wilkie.

As Wilkie pinned Leo and Morris against the wall, Fletch came close to them.

Leo could feel the heat of his rotten-smelling breath. Fletch grabbed Papa's hat from Leo's head and smacked Leo across the face with it. Hard.

"Your gold is long gone," he said, in his sickening growl.

Then he punched Morris in the stomach.

Morris doubled over, moaning in pain.

"Hey!" Leo said.

Without thinking, he gave Fletch a hard shove.

Fletch tripped and fell to the floor. In the faint predawn light, Leo saw the chilling stare on Fletch's face. It was the look of a rattlesnake ready to strike.

Fletch leaped to his feet and came charging toward Leo.

Leo closed his eyes and braced himself for a beating.

His entire body began to shake.

But wait.

He wasn't shaking.

The entire house was.

There was a strange sound, like thunder rumbling from deep in the ground.

The trembling got stronger. The noise rose up around them, so loud that it hurt Leo's ears.

The floor bounced beneath their feet.

"What is it?" Wilkie said.

Morris grabbed Leo by the arm.

"It's an earthquake!" Morris shouted. "We have to get out of here!"

CHAPTER 8

But Leo couldn't run. The shaking was too strong. The floor rose and fell, tossing Leo into the air and dropping him. Plaster rained down from the ceiling and swirling dust filled Leo's nose, eyes, and mouth.

The noise grew louder. It sounded like a hundred freight trains were rushing through the house, their whistles screaming. The shaking stopped for a few seconds, and Leo managed to stand up. He staggered a few steps toward the front door. But the shaking started up again, stronger than before. Fletch rushed past him. Leo saw him dive through the front doorway.

The rumbling became stronger still. Leo fell again. Now the entire building seemed to be rising and falling, twisting and turning.

Smack! Something hit him on the back, hard.

And then another — *thud* — hit him in the shoulder.

Bricks. They were falling from the ceiling. That huge chimney was collapsing.

Leo had to get out! But he couldn't even stand. He curled himself into a ball, sure he was about to be buried alive.

Suddenly he felt hands gripping his arm. Someone was pulling him forward.

Morris!

They rushed together and leaped toward the door. They landed hard on the sidewalk. And then:

Crack!

Boom!

Bricks poured down, hundreds of them, spilling out the door.

Had they been just a few steps slower, they both would have been buried.

The ground gave one last great shake.

And then it stopped.

The earth was still.

The silence was almost as frightening as the noise had been. Leo lay on his stomach, afraid to move or even to take a breath.

Now what would happen? He'd never been through an earthquake before. He felt sure the shaking would start again.

Morris was right next to him. His face was streaked with dirt and sweat. He had an angry bump just below his eye. Like Leo, he seemed too stunned to speak.

Leo looked in shock at the scene around them.

Was this really the neighborhood he'd been

walking through just minutes before? It looked like a furious giant had marched through the city, jumping over some houses and stomping on others. Bricks, stones, and glass covered the sidewalks and spilled into the street. Some of the rickety houses had collapsed. Others looked like a sneeze would send them crashing down.

People stood on the sidewalks, terrified. Families huddled together. Babies broke the silence with screams. Some people were stretched across the sidewalks, not moving.

Leo looked around at all the crumbled buildings. How many people were trapped? There had to be hundreds buried alive.

Or dead.

Fletch and Wilkie were nowhere to be seen.

Fear rose up in Leo. What would he do now? Where would he go?

It had been hard enough for him to get by on his own before.

How would he survive in this ruined city?

His mind swirled with worry. He imagined himself wandering the ruined streets, scrounging for food like a rat. Not even Grandpop had faced anything like this.

Morris turned to him with a thoughtful expression. "No wonder the dogs were howling," he said.

"What?" Leo said.

"The dogs. Did you hear them howling last night? Animals can sense earthquakes before they happen. They can feel the vibrations of the earth deep underground. I read all about it in a book."

Was Morris serious? Was he really talking about a book as they sat in the middle of an earthquake? This kid was unbelievable!

Leo stood up and shook the plaster from his hair. The ground started to rumble again.

Leo froze, and braced himself.

A crash echoed from down the street—another building caving in.

And just as suddenly, the shaking stopped again.

"Aftershocks," Morris said. "The ground is going to keep moving for days."

Was there anything Morris didn't know?

People were shouting behind them.

"Fire!" a man said.

A plume of black smoke rose from one of the collapsed houses.

"We have to get out of here," Morris said. "I smell gas. The quake has broken the gas lines. This whole hill is going to be burning within an hour."

Leo shuddered. Nothing scared him more than fire.

He thought of the fire that Grandpop had lived through in the Sierra Mountains. That was the closest Grandpop came to dying on his journey west. The story scared Leo so much that Papa had only told it a few times.

"Where should we go?" Leo said.

"I'm not sure," Morris said. "We need to get away from here. We should head west, toward Golden Gate Park."

"What about your uncle?" Leo said.

A shadow seemed to pass through Morris's eyes. "He left the city days ago," the younger kid said. "Something about a poker game."

"You don't know where he went?"

Morris shook his head.

No wonder he was always waiting for Leo to come home. He was all by himself.

"Some uncle," Leo said.

"That's all right," Morris said, matter-of-factly. "I have you."

The swirling in Leo's mind suddenly stopped.

Morris looked right into Leo's eyes, and Leo looked right back.

As usual, Morris was right. He did have Leo.

And Leo had Morris.

Morris, the most annoying kid in the world. Morris, who had come looking for him in the dark. Morris, who had probably saved Leo's life by helping him escape from the saloon.

Maybe Morris wasn't very big. Maybe he didn't know when to shut up. But he was smart and tough. And he was the truest friend Leo had ever had.

"That's right," Leo said.

Morris nodded, like they'd struck a deal. "Let's go," he said.

But as they were walking by the saloon, something in the rubble caught Leo's eye.

At first he thought it might be a rat crawling out from under the bricks.

But no.

It was a hand.

CHAPTER 9

It had to be Wilkie.

Leo had seen Fletch dive out the door. But not Wilkie.

He must have gotten caught in that shower of bricks.

Leo's heart pounded. Just a few minutes ago he would have prayed for Wilkie Barnes to get buried in a heap of rubble. But now he and Morris rushed over and started grabbing bricks off the pile on top of the bully.

The air was getting smokier. But Leo and Morris kept working until finally they could see Wilkie. He was turned on his side, his face hidden.

Morris gently put his fingers against Wilkie's throat. "He's alive," Morris said. "I can tell that."

But Wilkie still wasn't moving. And he was pinned under two huge roof beams.

They formed an X over his body, protecting him from being completely crushed under the bricks. The beams had probably saved his life. But now they were like a cage that trapped him. Leo and Morris tried to lift one of the beams, but it was too heavy.

Leo looked around and saw that a house three doors down was on fire. Flames reached out of the windows, like bright orange arms trying to grab the houses all around it.

Soon the street would be one huge fire.

Leo had no idea what they should do. How could they leave Wilkie here, knowing he was alive? But if they stayed, the fire would kill them too!

Suddenly, Wilkie lifted his head.

With a mighty push, he knocked one of the beams away. His face, covered with dust, was stark white. Blood oozed from a gash on his forehead.

He really did look like a monster.

Leo and Morris watched in shock as Wilkie rose out of the rubble, tossing bricks aside like they were puffs of cotton. He stood up, dusted himself off, and looked around like he'd just woken up from a deep sleep.

"Is Fletch alive?" he asked.

"He got out," Leo said.

Wilkie sighed in relief.

But then he looked around.

"Then where is he?" he asked. "Where's Fletch?"

"He left," Morris said.

"He didn't try to get me out? He just took off without me?"

Morris and Leo looked at each other.

Neither wanted to say the truth: that Fletch had left Wilkie for dead in the rubble.

But Wilkie figured this out. His expression suddenly changed to fury. He picked up a brick and hurled it toward the pile of rubble that had been the saloon. He did it again, and again, and again. His eyes bulged. He grunted and growled like the rabid dogs that roamed the alleys.

And then finally Wilkie slumped down onto the ground, out of breath.

He looked up at Leo and Morris. His eyes, set deep in his chubby face, were filled with confusion. His lip quivered, and Leo thought he might burst into tears.

"When I was at that work camp in Seattle, a man came and said I should play football," Wilkie said. "There's a fancy school up there, where rich kids go. And he said I could go for free, that he'd teach me everything I needed to know. He said I could be a champion. But I wouldn't go! Because I'd never leave Fletch. I went to jail because of Fletch. I stuck by him all these years. And where did it get me? Under that pile of bricks."

Leo had no idea what to say.

But Morris did. "Come with us," he offered.

Wilkie looked at Morris and then at Leo.

Leo got the idea that Wilkie had never really seen them before.

He wiped the tears from his face and took a deep breath.

He picked himself up.

"We should get your gold back," he said.

"Fletch said it was gone," said Leo.

"Never believe Fletch," Wilkie said. "He has it. And I know where he went."

Leo looked at Morris.

"Let's go," Morris said.

CHAPTER 10

Wilkie led them back toward Market Street.

Wilkie was sure Fletch had gone back to the abandoned house where they stashed their loot.

"That way if the police got us," he explained, "they wouldn't find it."

They zigzagged through the crowds of people. Most of them were heading away from where Wilkie was taking them. And no wonder. The damage was worse the farther south they walked. One boardinghouse was split in half. Another had been swallowed by the earth almost to its rooftop. Trolley tracks were twisted like pretzels. On one block, men were trying to hoist a horse out of a hole in the street.

Leo tried not to look at the collapsed buildings, but he couldn't stop thinking about who might still be inside.

The fires were worse down here. With every step the smoke was thicker, the air hotter. Leo's lungs started to ache.

They were about to cross Market Street when a fire wagon clattered up and stopped in front of them. The two huge horses pulling the wagon wheezed and snorted. Sweat soaked their bodies. Two firefighters jumped off, dragging a thick hose. They hooked it up to a hydrant, but only a trickle of water came out.

A man in a bloodstained shirt rushed up to the firemen.

"Please help me," he begged. "Everything I own is in my house, and a fire is moving toward it."

He pointed across the street, where the roof of one house was on fire. Next door, men were leading horses out of a stable.

"I'm sorry sir," said the taller of the firemen. "The quake broke our water mains. We've been up and down Market. We can't find any water to fight the fires."

"You're just going to let the city burn?" the man exclaimed.

The firemen said nothing. But their eyes — weary and scared — told the answer.

San Francisco was burning. And nobody could stop it.

The firemen rolled up their hoses, climbed into their wagon, and continued down the street.

Leo knew they should get out of here. Morris was right.

But suddenly Morris gasped.

"It's Fletch!" he cried, pointing across the street.

Leo saw him. He was carrying a small, tattered flour sack.

"Fletch!" shouted Wilkie.

His voice boomed through the smoky air.

Fletch turned, took one look at Wilkie, and bolted down the alley next to the burning house.

To Leo's amazement, it wasn't Wilkie who took off first after Fletch.

It was Morris.

They both disappeared into the alley.

Leo and Wilkie started after them.

But they had barely crossed the street when the ground jolted with another aftershock.

People screamed and ran into the street.

There was a deep cracking noise right above them.

A piece of rooftop from the burning house crashed onto the sidewalk. Garbage on the ground erupted into flames. The alley was now blocked by a wall of fire.

CHAPTER 11

Leo stepped toward the alley.

Wilkie grabbed him by the back of the shirt.

"No," he said. "There's no way out of there!"

"What do you mean?"

"That alley doesn't cut through," he said.

"How do you know?" Leo said.

"I know every alley in this town," Wilkie said. "That one is useless."

But Leo had to do something. He couldn't let Morris die in that alley.

How could he help? Leo searched his mind for ideas. And as usual, his thoughts turned to Grandpop.

He remembered that terrifying story of the forest fire in the Sierras. He'd only heard it a few times. But he remembered every detail.

Grandpop had finally crossed into California. In just a few more days, he'd be in gold country. He'd left his horse and wagon at a trading post. He'd headed up into the woods to hunt for rabbits. He would need their skins to trade for gold-mining tools.

It had been a hot and dry summer. Everywhere he looked there were dying trees, their leaves brown and papery. Dead grass and weeds crunched under Grandpop's boots.

There was hardly a speck of green anywhere.

Grandpop roamed the woods. He bagged a few rabbits.

And then clouds rolled in. Grandpop had

smiled up at the sky. A cool rain was just what he needed.

But only a few raindrops fell.

Meanwhile, lightning sliced through the sky.

And then —

KABOOM!

A lightning bolt struck a dead tree, turning it into a burning torch.

More lightning bolts shot out of the clouds, stabbing the ground like burning spears.

Soon there were fires everywhere.

A powerful wind fanned the flames. Within just a few minutes, Grandpop was stuck in the middle of a ring of fire.

The heat was so strong that the metal on his belt started to melt.

Grandpop had no idea what to do.

He got down on his hands and knees. Down low the smoke wasn't as thick, and he could see where he was going.

He almost didn't see the stream until he'd crawled into it.

It was practically dry, with just a few inches of water covering the muddy bottom. But there was enough so that Grandpop could lie down and soak his clothes. He took his kerchief and drenched it in water.

He put the soaking kerchief over his head, filled his lungs with air, and dashed through the flames.

Seconds later, when he came out the other side, his pants and the back of his coat were on fire.

He rolled into the dirt and put them out.

Then he ran for his life.

When he staggered back into the trading post, nobody recognized him. His beard and eyebrows were singed off. His face was black with ash, his fingers blistered red.

But once again, his quick thinking and calm head had saved him.

"I need to find some water," Leo said to Wilkie now.

"You heard those firemen," Wilkie said. "They can't even find any."

Leo thought for a minute. He remembered the men leading those horses out of the stable.

Where there were horses, he thought, there had to be water.

Wilkie followed Leo as he dashed into the stable.

Sure enough, there was a trough filled with dirty water.

There was also a blanket.

Wilkie watched as Leo climbed into the trough of water and soaked himself from head to toe. Then he soaked the blanket so it was dripping wet.

"What are you doing?" Wilkie said.

"This water is going to protect me," Leo said, out of breath, "when I run into the alley."

"You can't go in there," Wilkie said. "That little bit of water isn't going to do anything."

"I'll make it," Leo said. "I'll make it."

He repeated those words in his mind, trying to believe them, as he ran back outside. At the entrance to the alley, Leo put the blanket around his body and over his head.

And then Wilkie grabbed him again.

"Let go!" Leo shouted. They had no time to waste!

But Wilkie wasn't trying to stop him.

"I'm going with you," he said.

Leo opened his mouth to tell Wilkie no, to tell him to stay where he was.

But there wasn't time to argue. And from the look in Wilkie's eyes, he understood that there was no stopping Wilkie.

They were in this together.

Leo had to stand on his tiptoes to get the blanket around Wilkie. "Make sure your face is covered," Leo told him. "On the count of three, take a deep breath and run as fast as you can!"

Leo filled his lungs and put the blanket over their heads.

"One, two, three!"

Leo and Wilkie rushed into the fire.

CHAPTER 12

Their leap through the flames took just seconds.

But Leo knew that for as long as he lived, he would never forget the feeling of that scorching heat. The fire seemed to pull at the blanket like a beast hungry for Leo's flesh.

When they came out, Wilkie's pant leg was on fire. "Look out!" Leo called.

Leo grabbed the blanket and patted out the flames.

They looked at each other in shock: They'd made it!

But still, the smoke was thick, and it hurt to breathe.

"Do you see him?" Leo shouted.

"I can barely see anything," Wilkie said.

Leo remembered Grandpop, crawling through the brush looking for the stream.

"Get down," Leo said, dropping to his knees.

The air was clearer closer to the ground. But the heat was searing. The wall of fire roared behind them.

People shouted from the street.

"Get out!"

"It's all burning!"

"It's too late!"

They had just a minute or two to find Morris and get out, Leo knew.

Bits of glass from shattered windows cut into Leo's hands and knees as he crawled. His heart pounded with fear. He felt dizzy from the smoke.

He and Wilkie screamed Morris's name.

But with the shouting of the crowd and the roaring of the fires, it was almost impossible to hear anything.

Until, finally, they heard a voice.

"Leo! Over here!"

The voice was weak.

Leo moved forward . . . and then his heart gave a wild jump.

All he could see was Morris's head, on the ground.

Only his head.

His body was gone.

Wilkie came up behind Leo and gasped. "What the . . ."

Leo almost jumped up and ran in horror.

But then he understood. Morris's head hadn't been cut off. He'd fallen into some kind of hole. Only his head and one arm were sticking out.

"I'm stuck," Morris said. "I can't breathe."

Wilkie rushed over and grabbed Morris's arm with both of his hands.

He gave a mighty tug. But Morris barely budged.

"It's tight in here," Morris said. "Go slow."

Inch by inch, Wilkie pulled Morris from the earth, like a farmer pulling a gigantic carrot from his garden.

With each second that passed, the crackling roar of the fire grew louder. Sweat poured off of Leo's body.

Wilkie finally got Morris out of the hole. Leo grabbed hold of Morris, who wobbled on his feet. He held on to Morris, even after Morris was steady.

"I'm okay," Morris said. "We need to get out."

Morris pointed to an open window just above a heap of garbage.

"That way," he said. "That's how Fletch got out. He knew I was stuck. I kept calling him. But he just kept going."

Anger rose up in Leo. But there was no time to think about Fletch now.

They all climbed up the heap of garbage. Wilkie got to the top first. He clambered through the window, and then reached out to help Morris and Leo get in.

They were in somebody's bedroom. A dresser had smashed down on top of the bed. It looked like it had dropped through a giant hole in the ceiling. Luckily it seemed that the person who lived here had escaped.

The heat was very strong, and Leo was sure that some of the rooms of this building were burning. He prayed they could make it down in time, before the fire reached them or the building collapsed on top of them.

They found the stairs and began to make their way down. They walked lightly. But with each step, the stairway swayed. The wood groaned and creaked. One small aftershock and this whole place would tumble to the ground.

Wilkie suddenly stopped short.

"Hurry, Wilkie," Leo said.

But then he saw it. A body was lying on the floor.

At first he thought it was the person who lived here.

But then came the rasping voice.

"Wilkie," the body groaned.

It was Fletch.

CHAPTER 13

Fletch looked at Wilkie with a sweet smile painted on his face. "I knew you'd find me, old pal. I knew it. I was sitting here praying. And here you are."

Fletch was clutching that white flour sack.

"Here," he said, holding it out to Wilkie. "See? I saved it for you. I was going to come look for you. I swear I was."

"Sure you were, Fletch," Wilkie said in a weak voice. "I know you didn't forget about me."

Leo and Morris looked at each other, unsure of what was happening.

Did Wilkie really believe Fletch's lies? Was he going to join back up with him?

"Come on," Fletch rasped. "We can share with your new buddies too, if that's what you want. Whatever you say, pal. Whatever you say."

"I'll take care of you, Fletch," Wilkie said.

His voice didn't sound weak anymore.

"Of course you will," Fletch said. "We're a team, you and me. We take care of each other."

Wilkie snatched the flour sack from Fletch. He handed it to Leo.

"Your gold is in there," he said. "Take it."

"Sure," Fletch said. "Sure thing. Let the kid have his gold back. We're all friends now."

Leo rummaged through the sack. It was filled with money—bills and coins, watches and wallets. He found his gold nugget. It felt warm, as though it had been in Papa's hand just moments before. He handed the flour sack back to Wilkie.

Wilkie stepped back and stared at Fletch.

"You left me for dead," Wilkie said.

"No!" Fletch cried. "I was coming back for you. That's where I was heading. I swear it."

Leo could see the rage on Wilkie's face. It was as though the heat and fury of the fire had taken control of him. Wilkie grabbed a splintered piece of wood. He raised it up, so it was over Fletch's head.

Leo and Morris both leaped forward.

"No, Wilkie!" they both shouted. They each grabbed one of Wilkie's massive arms.

Wilkie shook them off like they were butterflies.

He glared at Fletch. He was set to smash that wood over Fletch's head.

But Morris moved so that he was between Fletch and Wilkie.

"We don't have time for this," Morris said, in his matter-of-fact voice. "We have to go."

Leo stood frozen, afraid that Wilkie might hurt Morris. Then what would happen?

But somehow Morris could always get people to pay attention, whether they wanted to or not.

Leo reached up and took hold of the wood. Wilkie held it tight, but finally he let Leo take it.

Wilkie grabbed Fletch roughly by the arm and stood him up.

Fletch cried out in pain. Leo could see that his leg was horribly twisted. He needed to get to a hospital.

Wilkie didn't care. He dragged Fletch, yelling and limping, out into the street and tossed him onto the sidewalk.

There were two policemen just up the street.

"Maybe they'll help you," Wilkie said.

Then he spat on the ground and stormed away.

Leo and Morris hurried after him.

None of them looked back at Fletch.

But they could hear his rasping cries echoing behind them.

They'd walked just a few blocks when they passed a woman standing in front of a ruined, burning house. Her four little children were gathered around her, their clothes tattered and covered with ash.

The woman was sobbing to a soldier.

"I've lost everything!" she wailed. "My husband! My house! Everything! What will we do? What will become of me and my children?"

The soldier patted the woman's arm but then moved on.

Wilkie stopped short. He went to the woman. Without a word, he handed her the flour sack. Then he turned and hurried back to Leo and Morris.

Leo could see that Wilkie's face had changed. The blazing look was gone. A peaceful look had come over him. He didn't look back at the

woman. But Leo did. He watched her open the bag and look in. Leo knew he'd never forget the look of amazement on her face.

With every hour they walked, they heard of new fires, new neighborhoods destroyed—all of the streets south of Market, Rincon Hill, downtown, Chinatown. City Hall was gone. So was the library, with its one million books.

Morris got tears in his eyes when he heard that.

Hundreds of little fires had joined together into huge firestorms that raced through the city. No neighborhood was safe. And so they just kept walking.

Leo had never been so tired. Or thirsty. His entire body ached. His eyes burned. He had cuts all over his hands. He had no idea where they'd end up.

But he was still in one piece. That was something.

He had his gold nugget back.

And he had a feeling inside, one he hadn't felt since Papa was still alive.

Walking between Wilkie and Morris, his shoulders brushing theirs, he knew in his heart that he wasn't alone.

CHAPTER 14

APRIL 21, 1906
SACRAMENTO, CALIFORNIA

Leo stood on the train platform at the Sacramento station.

The sun shone brightly in the clear blue sky. Beside him, Morris had his face turned up, enjoying the fresh, clear air.

All around them were refugees from San Francisco. There were all different kinds of

people—fancy ladies and street kids, Chinese families and scruffy gamblers, businessmen and very old people. Coats and hats were covered with ash and dust. Some people wore bandages, or walked with crutches. And they all shared the same expression, a mixture of shock and relief.

Their city was gone.

Thousands were dead.

But they had escaped. Alive.

They'd gotten to the California capital just that morning: Leo, Morris, Wilkie, and thousands of strangers.

The Southern Pacific Railroad had given out one free train ticket to anyone who wanted to leave San Francisco. After spending three miserable days in Golden Gate Park, the boys all wanted to get as far away from San Francisco as they could. The park had been turned into a tent city. Soldiers handed out food and water, but there wasn't enough for everyone. Leo and the guys had waited in line all day just to get a piece of bread and some water. Sleeping was impossible with all the crying and screaming.

The fires had finally gone out on the fourth morning after the earthquake. But smoke and ash still filled the sky. Every breath reminded Leo of what had happened.

Some people in the tent city were already talking about rebuilding.

A preacher had stood in front of a crowd, calling on the crowd not to give up on San Francisco.

"Our city is gone," he said. "But its spirit is here! We will rebuild!"

Leo believed it. Grandpop had helped build this city the first time, when it had been turned from a bunch of shacks in the mud into one of the most beautiful cities in the world.

But Leo knew that he needed to put the ruins and smoke behind him. Even before the quake, he'd been looking for a fresh start. Wilkie and Morris needed one too.

They'd left Golden Gate Park and walked for three hours through the smoldering ruins to get to the train station. They'd crowded onto the first train they could. Five hours later they were breathing in clear air, gazing up at buildings that stood strong and tall. The earth was still.

They figured they'd stay in Sacramento. They'd sell newspapers. They'd share a room. They'd get by.

But over these past few hours, their plans had changed.

That morning, the three of them had gone to a bank. Within the hour, Leo had sold his gold nugget.

It's what Grandpop would have done, he was sure.

And what Papa would have wanted Leo to do.

He had enough money to buy Wilkie a train ticket to Seattle.

Wilkie was going to find that man who wanted to turn him into a football star.

"Why don't you guys come with me?" Wilkie had said. "You could play too. We could all be on the same team."

"We already are," Morris said in that wise voice of his.

They all smiled. They were some team, the three of them.

Leo had the idea they always would be, no matter where life took them.

But Leo and Morris weren't going with Wilkie. They had a plan of their own.

Leo had bought two tickets to New York City.

He and Morris would find Morris's cousins.

They would start new lives there.

It was a crazy idea, Leo knew.

But no crazier than when Grandpop had left New Hampshire to make his fortune in gold country.

Wilkie took a long look at them before he got onto the train, like he was painting their pictures in his mind.

"I'll see you again," he said.

He stuck his hand out, and Leo and Morris put their hands on top of his. Their fingers were cut up, black with ash and grime, scraped raw in spots. But their hands looked strong, especially put all together.

The train whistle blew. And then, just as when he gave that sack of loot to the crying lady, Wilkie turned and hurried off without another word.

Leo and Morris stood in silence, watching Wilkie's train disappear.

They bought themselves some cold bottles of milk and warm rolls.

And then there was nothing to do but wait for their own train.

Leo felt in his pocket where the gold nugget used to be.

"Do you miss your gold?" Morris asked quietly.

"No, I don't," Leo said. The words came out quickly, and Leo was surprised to hear them.

But no, he didn't miss it.

It was taking Leo and Morris where they needed to go.

And Papa had given him other treasures, he realized.

Priceless treasures.

All of those stories about Grandpop.

And the belief Leo had in his own luck and courage.

That came from Papa too, a faith stronger and shinier than gold.

And now, as he waited for his train, Leo heard Papa's words, brighter and clearer than ever.

Something remarkable was going to happen to him.

He could feel it.

MY SAN FRANCISCO STORY

I'm writing this letter from San Francisco, from a desk that overlooks the San Francisco Bay. I visit this city often. But this trip was different: This time, I came with my husband and kids to retrace Leo's journey. We went high up on Rincon Hill, roaming the crowded neighborhoods south of Market Street, exploring the grassy hills of Golden Gate Park. Each morning, we woke up to a gray blanket of San Francisco fog and the clang of the cable car bells.

Like all of the I Survived books, this story is a work of historical fiction. The facts are true, and all of the places I wrote about really exist. The characters come from my imagination.

But I spend so much time with the characters I write about that I start thinking they're real. Throughout this visit, I kept hoping I would catch sight of Leo and Morris sitting on a front stoop. Peering into the dark alleys south of Market Street, I half expected to see Fletch and Wilkie up to their old tricks.

I also kept my eyes open for scars of the earthquake and fire of 1906. But all I could find was one beautiful memorial to the heroic firefighters of that day. I guess it's not surprising that the people of San Francisco would want to forget that terrible time. Three thousand people died in the earthquake and fire of 1906. Eighty percent of the city was destroyed.

Back then, many predicted that San Francisco would never recover. But within three years, there were 20,000 new buildings. A decade after the disaster, the city was even grander than before.

Still, every San Franciscan knows that danger lurks below the earth's surface. This beautiful city is part of one of the most earthquake-prone regions in the world. A strong earthquake hit here in 1989, damaging many buildings and bridges and killing 63 people. Scientists predict that a stronger quake will happen one day, though nobody can predict exactly when.

This thought haunted me as I walked around with my family.

But in the end, I decided it was best not to think about hidden and hopefully distant dangers. Instead I thought about Leo and Morris, and how happy they would be to know that San Francisco rose up from the ashes of 1906 to become the thriving city it is today.

This photo looking down Sacramento Street in San Francisco was taken by Arnold Genthe on April 18, 1906.

Sacramento Street today.

QUESTIONS AND ANSWERS ABOUT EARTHQUAKES

How strong was the San Francisco earthquake?

Back in 1906, the science of earthquakes (called **seismology**) was just beginning. There were no instruments to measure earthquakes. Today, earthquake scientists, called **seismologists**, use the moment magnitude scale (MMS) to determine the strength of an earthquake. The earthquake that hit northeastern Japan in March 2011 measured 9.0 on the MMS. Any earthquake 9.0

or above is considered catastrophic. Earthquakes below 6.0 are considered moderate. Experts estimate that the San Francisco earthquake was far less powerful than the Japan quake, and would have measured a 7.9 on the MMS. This is still considered very strong. However, in San Francisco, the fires caused more damage than the earthquake itself.

Why do earthquakes happen?

The entire surface of the earth is covered with a thick layer of rock called the **crust.** The crust is many miles thick. It is broken up into about 18 gigantic pieces, like the pieces of a puzzle. These pieces of crust, called **tectonic plates**, are always moving, slowly sliding and bumping into each other. The edges of the plates are rough, and sometimes when they slide against each other, they get stuck together. Pressure builds and builds, sometimes for many years. And then suddenly the pressure gets so strong that the pieces get unstuck with a sudden violent movement. This is the moment that earthquakes happen.

Where do most earthquakes happen?

Eighty percent of the world's earthquakes happen in an area surrounding the Pacific Ocean nicknamed the "ring of fire." This area has more than 450 active volcanoes. And it sits on top of the Pacific plate, a huge tectonic plate under the Pacific Ocean. The Pacific plate is always moving, crashing into other plates and causing more earthquakes than any other. The movement of the Pacific plate caused recent powerful earthquakes in Chile, New Zealand, and Japan. It also caused the San Francisco earthquake of 1906.

What was the strongest earthquake ever recorded?

The strongest earthquake ever recorded happened in 1960 in Chile. It measured 9.5 on the MMS. The *deadliest* earthquake on record happened in central China, in the year 1556. It struck a region where most people lived in caves carved into soft rock. The earthquake caused the caves to collapse. An estimated 830,000 people died.

OTHER EARTHQUAKE FACTS

- The most earthquake-prone state
  in the United States is Alaska.
  That's where America's strongest
  earthquake occurred, a quake
  measuring 9.2 that hit Prince
  William Sound on March 28, 1964.
- Earthquakes happen throughout the
  United States, though most are
  so small people can't feel them.
  The only states that have not

had earthquakes in recent years
are Wisconsin, Florida, Iowa, and
North Dakota.

- Every year, 10,000 earthquakes
  occur in Southern California.
  Most are so mild that people do
  not feel them.

- **Tsunamis** are giant waves caused
  by earthquakes beneath the ocean
  floor.

- Earthquakes even happen on the
  moon. They are called **moonquakes.**

Lucas sat on the bench, waiting for Dad.

Taxis zoomed past and bikers wove between buses and cars. Men and women rushed to work with determined looks. A woman hurried by with a stroller. The little girl riding inside smiled and waved at Lucas.

Lucas waved back. And for the first time in two weeks, he smiled too.

He hadn't wanted to come into the city for the day. He'd wanted to stay in his room, in the dark, by himself. Dad had to practically drag him out of bed and into the truck. For almost two hours in rush-hour traffic, Lucas hadn't said a word.

But sitting here, in the middle of the morning crowd, he started to forget about his troubles. Another first in the past two weeks — for a moment he wasn't worried about his concussion, or that he'd never play football again, and that his life was somehow over before he'd even turned twelve.

Where had those worries gone?

He thought of what Mom had said that morning, warning him to keep an eye on his wallet.

"Watch out, or some crook will pick it right from your pocket," she'd said as she kissed him good-bye.

Maybe that's what happened to his worries. Someone had plucked them from his pocket.

They could keep them, he decided.

He looked up into the cloudless sky. He couldn't remember a day so bright and clear, a sky so blue.

But then something caught his eye — a glint of metal.

And then there was a roaring sound.

Out of nowhere, a huge jet airplane came into view above the buildings.

Lucas stood up.

He had never seen an airplane flying so low, except right near the airports.

He could see it so clearly—the engines on the wings, the sun glinting off the windows. He could even read the words on the side: American Airlines.

That plane had to be in trouble. It was going to crash!

Or could it be that airplanes flew like this all the time over New York City?

No. Something was wrong. People up and down the sidewalk had stopped in their tracks. All eyes were on the sky.

Dad appeared and grabbed Lucas by the arm.

"What on earth—?" he said.

The plane turned slightly, and the engine's roar got louder. It was speeding up.

It was heading right for the Twin Towers.

"No!" someone shouted.

Kaboom!

A ball of fire exploded out of one of the buildings.

Lucas turned and hid his face in Dad's chest.

People screamed.

It can't be real, Lucas said to himself. *This isn't real.*

He didn't look back, afraid of what he would see.

He looked up at Dad instead. And the look he saw on Dad's face shook Lucas deep in his bones.

Dad had been a rescue fireman for ten years. He'd fought some of the worst fires in New York City. Nothing scared him. Except—Lucas had seen it—for a split second, the look of fear and shock in Dad's eyes.

And Lucas knew something else. Nothing was going to keep his dad away from that fire. There had to be thousands of people trapped in that tower.

And no matter how dangerous it was, it was Dad's job to try to save them.

I SURVIVED

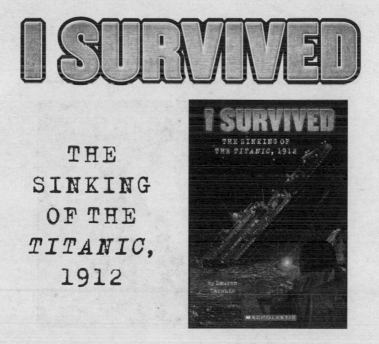

THE SINKING OF THE TITANIC, 1912

UNSINKABLE. UNTIL ONE NIGHT...

George Calder must be the luckiest kid alive. He and his little sister, Phoebe, are sailing with their aunt on the *Titanic*, the greatest ship ever built. George can't resist exploring every inch of the incredible boat, even if it keeps getting him into trouble.

Then the impossible happens—the *Titanic* hits an iceberg and water rushes in. George is stranded, alone and afraid, on the sinking ship. He's always gotten out of trouble before . . . but how can he survive this?

I SURVIVED

THE SHARK ATTACKS OF 1916

THERE'S SOMETHING IN THE WATER...

Chet Roscow is finally feeling at home in Elm Hills, New Jersey. He has a job with his uncle Jerry at the local diner, three great friends, and the perfect summertime destination: cool, refreshing Matawan Creek.

But Chet's summer is interrupted by shocking news. A great white shark has been attacking swimmers along the Jersey shore, not far from Elm Hills. Everyone in town is talking about it. So when Chet sees something in the creek, he's sure it's his imagination . . . until he comes face-to-face with a bloodthirsty shark!

I SURVIVED

HURRICANE KATRINA, 2005

HIS WHOLE WORLD IS UNDERWATER...

Barry's family tries to evacuate before Hurricane Katrina hits their home in the Lower Ninth Ward of New Orleans. But when Barry's little sister gets terribly sick, they're forced to stay home and wait out the storm.

At first, Katrina doesn't seem to be as severe a storm as forecasters predicted. But overnight the levees break, and Barry's world is literally torn apart. He's swept away by the floodwaters, away from his family. Can he survive the storm of the century—alone?

I SURVIVED

THE BOMBING OF PEARL HARBOR, 1941

A DAY NO ONE WILL EVER FORGET...

Ever since Danny's mom moved him to Hawaii, away from the dangerous streets of New York City, Danny has been planning to go back. He's not afraid of the crime or the dark alleys. And he's not afraid to stow away on the next ship out of Pearl Harbor.

But that morning, the skies fill with fighter planes. Bombs pound the harbor. Bullets rain down on the beaches. Danny is shocked — and, for the first time, he is truly afraid. He's a tough city kid. But can Danny survive the day that will live in infamy?